For my parents.
Junia Wonders

For my happy boy.
Daniela Volpari

Published by Gmür Verlag

Text copyright © 2014 Junia Wonders
Illustrations copyright © 2014 Gmür Verlag
All rights reserved.

ISBN 978-1495416743

The Roll-Away Pumpkin

Junia Wonders

Daniela Volpari

On a windy autumn day,
Marla Little comes running down the hill yelling,
"Help! My giant pumpkin is **rolling away!**
Onward it goes, rolling and turning,
with no sign of **stopping!"**

"Watch out!" she yells
as her pumpkin rolls ahead
toward the farmer's shed.

"Diddle-dee-doo!
Oh, what shall I do?"

"**Hurry!** Let's go after it before it rolls any **farther**," offers the **farmer**.

"Watch out!" she yells
as her pumpkin rolls ahead
toward the baker's wagon.

"Diddle-dee-doo!
Oh, what shall I do?"

"**Hurry!**
Let's go after it
before it rolls any **farther**,"
offers the **baker**.

"Watch out!" she yells
as her pumpkin rolls ahead
toward the milkman's cart.

"Diddle-dee-doo!
Oh, what shall I do?"**

"**Hurry!** Let's go after it before it rolls any **farther**," offers the **milkman**.

"Watch out!" she yells
as her pumpkin rolls ahead
toward the butcher's shop.

"Diddle-dee-doo!
Oh, what shall I do?"

"Hurry! Let's go after it before it rolls any farther," offers the **butcher**.

"**Watch out!**" she yells
as her pumpkin rolls ahead
toward the parade marchers.

"Diddle-dee-doo!
Oh, what shall I do?"

"**Hurry!**
Let's go after it
before it rolls any farther,"
offer the **parade marchers**.

"Look! A giant pumpkin is leading the way!"

"This is the best **vegetable parade** ever!"

"**Hurry**," says a plump lady, "the marchers will be here soon!

Those marchers will be **hungry!** A feast we must make ready!"

"Diddle-dee-doo!
I know what to do!"

shouts Marla Little as her pumpkin
rolls toward the lady stirring
a very big cauldron on the lawn.

In one swift move,
she tips the cauldron forward
so her giant pumpkin rolls into it,
never to come out again.

Well, not until the most delicious
pumpkin soup is cooked
and served to everybody.